FROM THE AWARD-WINNING
"RUBY'S STUDIO: THE SIBLINGS SH

MILES IS A MIGHTY BROTHERSAURUS

Written by:
Samantha Kurtzman-Counter
& Abbie Schiller

Illustrated by:
Valentina Ventimiglia

THE MOTHER
COMPANY

MILES REALLY WANTED TO ENJOY HIS **DINO DAY!**

MOM, DAD AND **LITTLE MAX** CAME RUSHING INTO THE LIVING ROOM.

"MILES, ARE YOU OK? **WHAT HAPPENED?**"

"I'M FINE. I WAS JUST **TRYING** TO CATCH SCOTTY'S BALL."

AS MOM, DAD, SCOTTY AND MAX RUSHED OUT THE DOOR, MILES TOOK A GOOD LOOK AT THE TROPHIES SURROUNDING HIM. HE NOTICED THAT MOST OF THEM WERE SCOTTY'S, AND EVEN LITTLE MAX GOT A MEDAL IN GYMNASTICS.

BUT **NONE OF THEM WERE HIS.** NOT ONE.

MILES FELT HIS THROAT GETTING TIGHT, LIKE HE MIGHT START TO CRY.
"I MEAN, SCOTTY AND MAX ARE ALREADY **CHAMPIONS!** ALL WE DO IS RUSH AROUND TO THEIR GAMES AND PRACTICES, AND **NO ONE CARES AT ALL ABOUT WHAT I LIKE TO DO!**"

"WAIT! I'VE GOT A **GREAT IDEA!** I NEED TO FIND SOMETHING **I CAN DO REALLY WELL** SO I CAN WIN A LOT OF TROPHIES AND SHOW THEM ALL HOW **GREAT I AM!**"
"OK, TIGER - SHOW ME WHAT YOU HAVE IN MIND!"

FIRST, MILES TRIED HIS HAND AT **ART**. HIS FIRST SUBJECTS WERE RED FLOWERS, RED APPLES AND A RED BALL.

HIS BRUSH DASHED ACROSS THE CANVAS WITH FLOURISH. PERHAPS HE WOULD BE A **GREAT ARTIST!**

MILES REALIZED THAT HIS GRANDPA WAS RIGHT:
HE DIDN'T NEED TROPHIES OR MEDALS TO BE SPECIAL.
ALL HE NEEDED WAS TO BE HIMSELF.

THE END.

A NOTE TO PARENTS AND TEACHERS

Recent studies have shown that often even more than parents, siblings affect the way children perceive themselves and how they relate to others outside the home. Within most families, siblings will naturally take on specific roles. "The Funny One," "The High Achiever," "The Anxious One," "The Athlete," "The Popular One." However, these roles are often taken on by default, as a response to what the other siblings are doing rather than as a true expression of each child's identity. It can be difficult for children to find their own unique identity - their "true self" - while fighting a constant battle for parental attention and praise.

We created *Miles is a Mighty Brothersaurus* to help parents, caregivers and educators support children who are struggling to find their place within their family system. Young children often need guidance to find the confidence to just be themselves and trust that they will be loved no matter what. Miles feels acutely that his interests don't command the same kind of attention as his older and younger siblings'. But through Grandpa's helpful wisdom, Miles discovers that perhaps what's even more important is the confidence to know that you are worthy and special, no matter your interests or how much attention you get for them.

Our aim at *The Mother Company* is to help children find their voice and empower them with the social and emotional tools they need to navigate the ups and downs of childhood. Through *Miles is a Mighty Brothersaurus*, we hope children will enjoy and relate to Miles's experience and glean a stronger sense of self-worth as a result.

Abbie Schiller & Samantha Kurtzman-Counter
The Mother Company Mamas

Dedicated to "Helping Parents Raise Good People," The Mother Company offers award-winning children's books, videos, apps, activity kits, events, parenting resources and more. Join us at TheMotherCo.com

THE MOTHER COMPANY